This Is the Van That Dad Cleaned

This Is the Van That Dad Cleaned

Lisa Campbell Ernst

Simon & Schuster Books for Young Readers

New York   London   Toronto   Sydney

SIMON & SCHUSTER BOOKS FOR YOUNG READERS

An imprint of Simon & Schuster Children's Publishing Division

1230 Avenue of the Americas, New York, New York 10020

Book design by Lucy Ruth Cummins

The text for this book is set in Filosofia.

The illustrations for this book are rendered in pastel, ink, and pencil.

Manufactured in China

10 9 8 7 6 5 4 3 2 1

Library of Congress Cataloging-in-Publication Data

Ernst, Lisa Campbell.

This is the van that Dad cleaned / Lisa Campbell Ernst.— 1st ed.

p. cm.

Summary: In the style of a classic cumulative rhyme, the children undo
all of Dad's hard work cleaning the family car.

ISBN 0-689-86190-7

[1. Automobiles—Fiction. 2. Cleanliness—Fiction.
3. Stories in rhyme.] I. Title.

PZ8.3.E7897 Th 2005

[E]—dc22

2003022052

first
edition

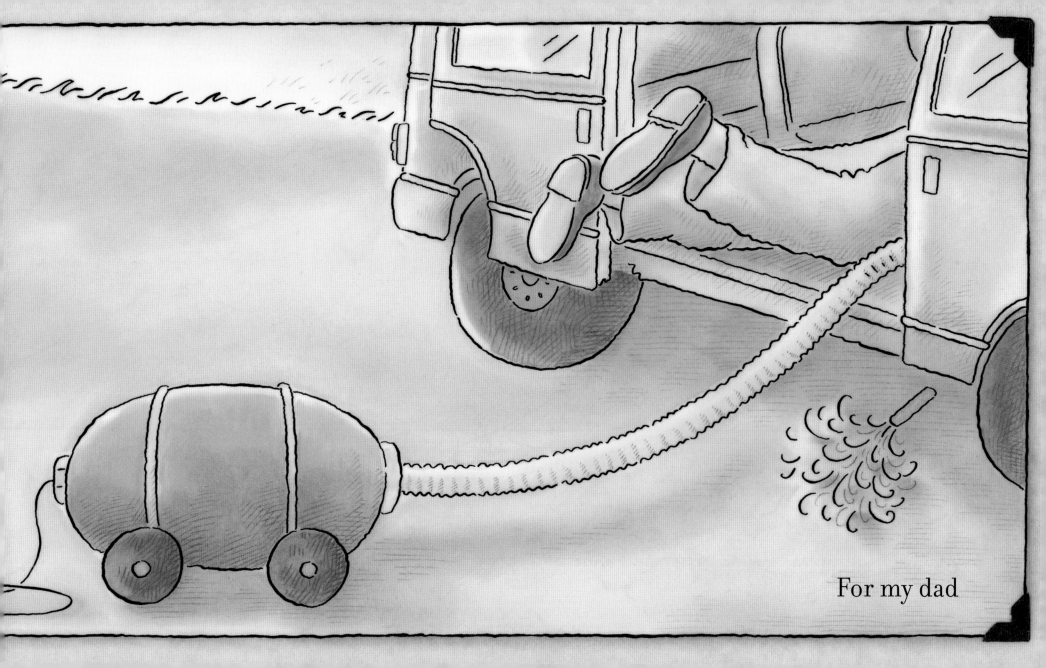

For my dad

This is the van
that Dad cleaned.

This is the girl

that rode in the van
that Dad cleaned.

This is the boy

that teased the girl
that rode in the van
that Dad cleaned.

This is the toy

that thrilled the boy
that teased the girl
that rode in the van
that Dad cleaned.

This is the bag

that held the toy
that thrilled the boy
that teased the girl
that rode in the van
that Dad cleaned.

This is the baby,

all forlorn,
that toppled the bag
that held the toy
that thrilled the boy
that teased the girl
that rode in the van
that Dad cleaned.

This is the ketchup,

now airborne,
that squirted the baby, all forlorn,
that toppled the bag
that held the toy
that thrilled the boy
that teased the girl
that rode in the van
that Dad cleaned.

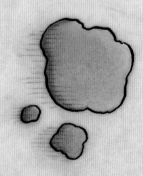

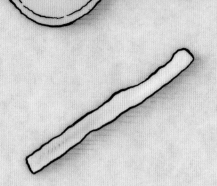

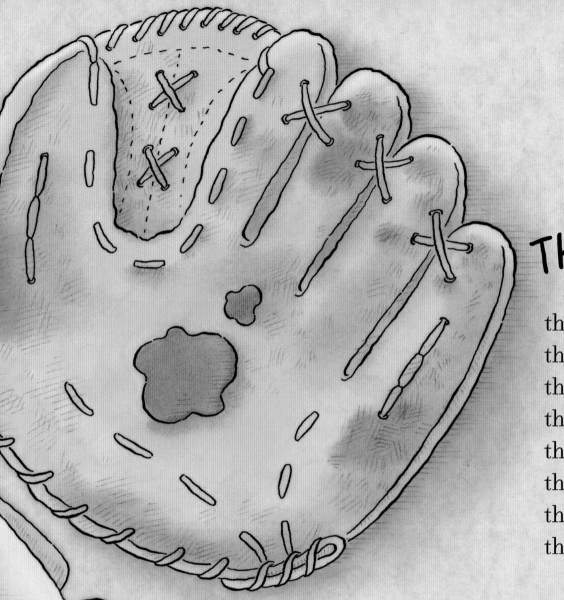

This is the glove,
so muddy and worn,
that squeezed the ketchup, now airborne,
that squirted the baby, all forlorn,
that toppled the bag
that held the toy
that thrilled the boy
that teased the girl
that rode in the van
that Dad cleaned.

This is the backpack,

tattered and torn,
that held the glove, so muddy and worn,
that squeezed the ketchup, now airborne,
that squirted the baby, all forlorn,
that toppled the bag
that held the toy
that thrilled the boy
that teased the girl
that rode in the van
that Dad cleaned.

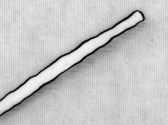

This is last Halloween's candy corn

that spilled from the backpack, tattered and torn,
that held the glove, so muddy and worn,
that squeezed the ketchup, now airborne,
that squirted the baby, all forlorn,
that toppled the bag
that held the toy
that thrilled the boy
that teased the girl
that rode in the van
that Dad cleaned.

This is the moose

with only one horn
that stuck to last Halloween's candy corn
that spilled from the backpack, tattered and torn,
that held the glove, so muddy and worn,
that squeezed the ketchup, now airborne,
that squirted the baby, all forlorn,
that toppled the bag
that held the toy
that thrilled the boy
that teased the girl
that rode in the van
that Dad cleaned.

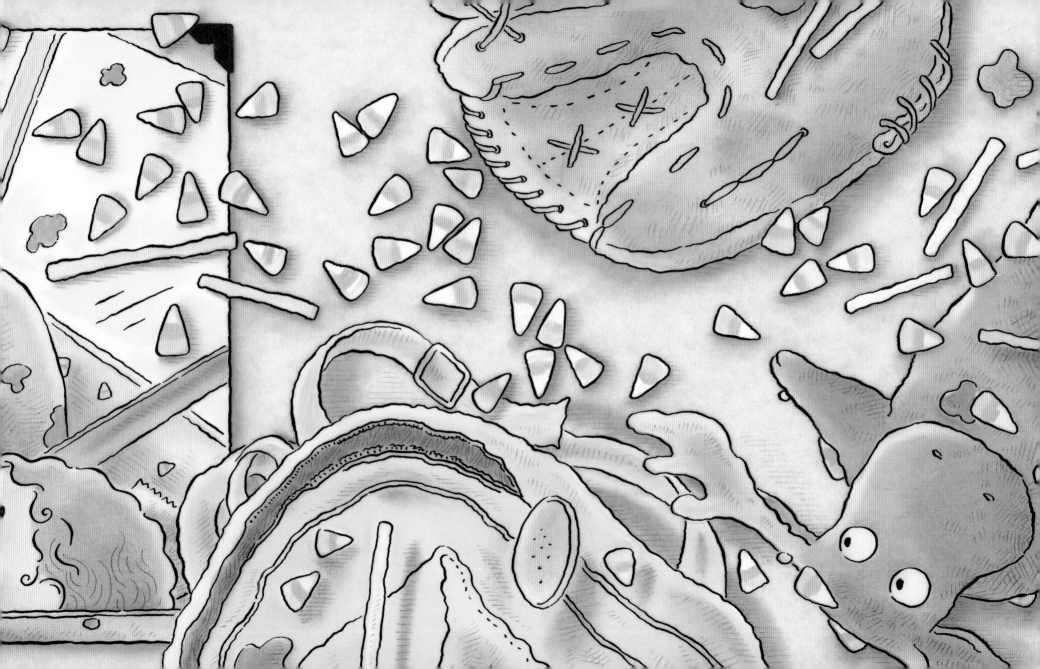

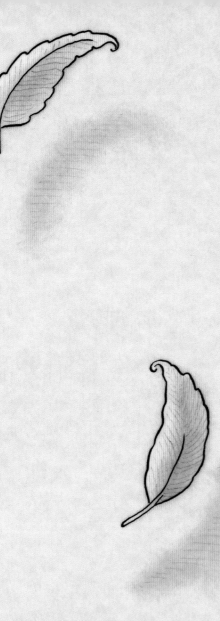

We are the kids,

early next morn,
that washed off the moose with only one horn,
and swept out last Halloween's candy corn,
and packed up the backpack all tattered and torn,
and cleaned up the glove so muddy and worn,
and scrubbed off the ketchup, once airborne,
and cheered up the baby, now adorned,
and picked up the bag
that held the toy
that thrilled the boy
that teased the girl
that rode in the van
that Dad cleaned.

This is the van that *we* cleaned!

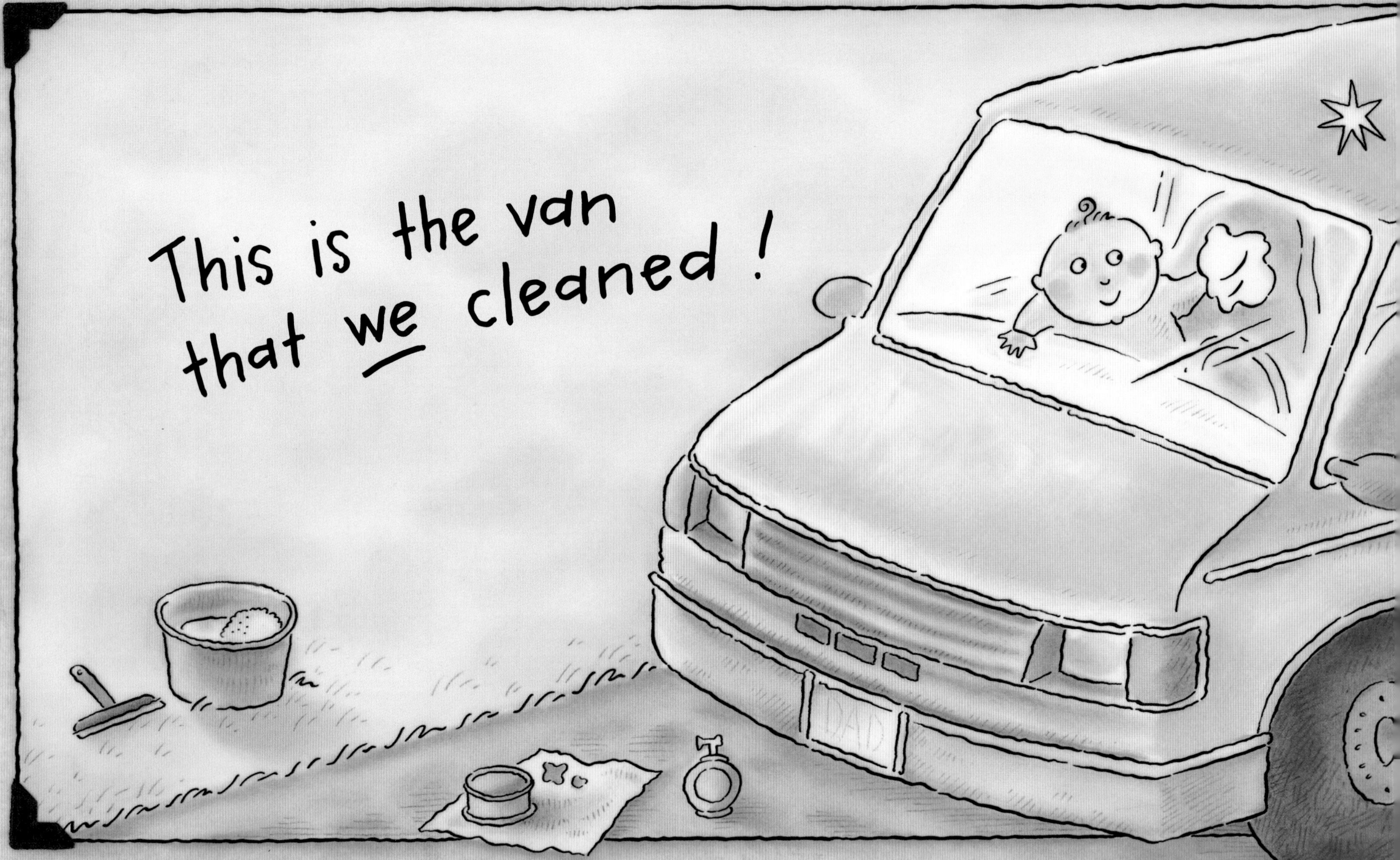